FOUR SHORT STORIES
ABOUT (but not for) CHILDREN

Henry Warren

Fall

Sugar

Capture the Flag

By George Clive Hook

ISBN 978-0-9820504-3-9
Hook Publishing
Unit 412
450 Village Green South
Lincolnshire, IL 60069

TABLE OF CONTENTS

Henry Warren--Left at the door steps of Episcopal Hall, a home for boys, by his mother, following the death of his father, frightened little Henry learns his lessons well on his way to becoming the self-confident Hank.

Fall (A *Christmas* Story)—When a simple, well intentioned experiment goes awry, will unexpected consequence be everlasting?

Sugar—The true story beyond the *Journey to the Ultimate Solution* and *The Children Saved*, which won Reagans for Genevieve Swag, the noted journalist!

Capture the Flag—Do the games boys play foretell the more deadly ones played by men and Nations?

HENRY WARREN

By George Hook

They had walked only a little over a mile. To Henry it had seemed much over. Then, of course, he neither knew nor could he be expected to know anything about the length of miles. But surely his mother knew the length in Lilliputian miles. They might have taken the Lawrence Avenue bus to Sacramento for twenty cents. Yet, if they had, Mr. Warren never could have come upon them—either to affirm or calm her doubts. She fully expected him to appear every step of the way. Not that Henry's mother believed in the Mystery of Black Cats or the Evil Eye; she merely believed in the power of a remarkable man to surmount death's barrier on behalf of his "loving wife" and his "immortality."

Mr. Warren did appear, but only in the many strangers who had passed without a word.

The two crossed more quickly over the city sewage canal because of an abrupt shift in the chill wind. Just beyond, they could see Episcopal Hall. Actually they could see three buildings surrounded by an old black iron gate. The one farthest from them was rectangular and of smooth red brick like a gymnasium. The one in the middle was long and tall with several flights of windows in neat rows across its rough grey face. The nearest and littlest was more like an ordinary home, a parsonage perhaps.

At this sight from the bridge Henry became urgently apprehensive. The end was near. The thought of leaving his mother's side frightened him tremendously, but not because he was afraid to go to bed with the lights off or without his teddy bear. He had and still looked forward to the adventure of a new school and making new friends. He had a premonition, however, that this adventure was about to be spoiled. He had a vague impression about being a sissy if he did not go beyond those big oak doors alone. But he knew too clearly that this true and sufficient reason in his eyes would be childish and insufficient in hers. Yet how ungrateful and unloving he would seem if he could give a reason for his wish!

Unfortunately, Henry was incapable of grafting domestic buds to foreign stems, and his attempt was enough to open the flood-gates of any mother's heart. Until this very moment his mother (not wanting in her knowledge of children) had intended to leave him at the door with Father Solomon in order to save Henry the embarrassment of a departure in front of the other boys. When she saw Henry on this verge of uncontrollable emotional chaos however, she immediately abandoned all thought of this mutual plan—separately arrived at—in favor of the more motherly one. And despite Henry's continuous pleading (and as a result of it) she went up the steps with him, into the Hall, and up to the dormitory with Father Solomon whose grim austerity did put Henry in mortal fear of leaving his mother's side at last, for reasons of darkness and teddy bears. In that dormitory where he was expected to live and in the midst of those boys whom he had hoped to befriend, Henry got the warmest (and most embarrassing) of motherly partings. So warm were these parting words and caresses that even the plump little arms of little Miss Cunningham could not stop the responding flood-gates of this child's heart for a full five minutes after his mother had gone.

When he did finally put his scrawny little fists to his eyes for the first time and looked on the world again, he met a wide-eyes circle of boys wearing pointed caps—no two the same color—and each menacingly holding a noisemaker. Henry looked into the housemother's face as she adjusted a funny little hat on his head and then put a crank in his hand.

"There now," she kissed him and scooted him off her abundant lap. His crank sounded and the circle, like the wall of a medieval castle, immediately answered in malevolent and echoing volleys.

There were more boys than Henry could count and he was introduced to them all by full name within a matter of minutes. Miss Cunningham then let them loose to make noise and play until the dinner bell rang.

Supper was an experience for Henry! Not only was the dining hall the biggest room he had ever seen, but it contained more chairs, more tables, more boys, more blinding lights and dazzling glass, plate and silver, and vibrated with much more noise than he had ever seen or heard in his short life. And because he was afraid that if for the least instant he appeared unoccupied his neighbors would tease him about the horrible scene he had so wanted to avoid, Henry ate more than he had ever eaten before. So much more that afterwards, when one of the fellows stood up—the one who looked to Henry so like a crafty red fox because of his freckles and dark red hair and later pleased Henry so much when he found out that his name was Fox—said a little something and then gave Miss Cunningham a big heart-shaped box with a big white bow, and when the other boys throughout the dining hall rose, Henry was so bloated and dizzy that he could not at first rise in the little space between the table and his chair and while trying to slide it back, he knocked it down. Only dread of reprisal kept him from crying.

Miss Cunningham reached over and kissed Fox, said he was "too good." She thanked everyone, said she "did not deserve such kindness from my boys," and shed a few tears as she expressed the wish that they would be as good and kind to the new housemother as they had been good and kind to her. Many of the boys reached for their napkins. Others made good use of their shirt sleeves. But Henry allowed no further embarrassment from that source.

By Breakfast the next day she was gone. In her place was Father Solomon. In place of the chatter and other noise which had so filled Henry with fear and foods was a ghostly quiet. Henry was afraid even to lift his fork for fear of rising out of anonymity before that austere form. Asking for the butter was beyond daring.

As embarrassment would have it, as calamity sometimes follows embarrassment, Henry fell under the wrong influence. Father Solomon had asked who would see Henry to school. The dumpy little boy sitting next to him had jumped up with his hand high. It was Alden, St. Bartholomew's outcast. No wonder! His appearance was repulsive. Instead of the usual, his skin was a jaundice yellow-green. Almost no hair grew on his head and when he opened his mouth to speak, a large black tooth always appeared. In short, Alden and a half-eaten unpitted olive would have been indistinguishable except for size and a few appendages. But Henry was unprejudiced by this resemblance. Furthermore, he had never seen an unpitted olive; only pimento-stuffed ones—and certainly that introduction of color spoiled the comparison completely.

Henry was introduced to the "Beaut," a precisely constructed "to scale model" of the latest navy submarine. Alden had just completed it. He considered it the best of his many works. But here again Henry had no means of comparison because the only other example of Alden's handicraft was a mustang fighter plane on the book case which had suffered from the wars which the rough hands of the boys in the dorm could have devised only for something of Alden's. All his other works had either been destroyed or were hidden.

So while the others played football or wrestled in the gym, Henry looked over Alden's plans for building "a precisely construct to scale model" of a German tank. Consequently, he knew none of the other boys; and he was unable to befriend them because he did not know their names. He did not know their names as a result of that unfortunate prior scene of departure between himself and his mother. But having been introduced once already he was too shy to admit by asking that he did not know them. He felt his asking would be an insult to them. As a result, the boys soon got the impression that Henry was just another Alden. They began to treat him accordingly.

Their favorite means of teasing was to hide his shoe or his shirt from him, or form a circle around him and play "keep away." But Henry, unlike Alden, thought these were games without malice (for a fact, he did not know what malice was) and had as much fun as they. He disliked only being shoved into his locker and things then being piled against the door to keep him in. He tolerated this without complaint, however, for fear that if he did complain all the other games would end. As this was the only attention paid him, its being stopped would be distasteful.

By the end of the week the boys had discerned that Henry was enjoying the "tease" and that as a result it was less effective against Alden. He never cried or screamed anymore. He even took the destruction of his new "Beaut" with equanimity. Hence, the tease was no longer any fun. But the remedy for that was simple enough to Charles Fox, who usually had led these raids on Alden's dignity. Without his leadership most of the boys would have given up teasing the two boys. But giving up under Fox was impossible. Giving up was cowardice, and no one was a "chicken;" giving up was stupid, and no one was a "stupe;" giving up was disloyal, and no one was a "traitor."

Johnny Raggety proposed that they forget about the tease because there was no longer any fun in it. Fox, stumping the crowded locker room in grand manner, let go with a streak of nouns and verbs that would have done credit to the most intimidating union organizer. He threatened to boil his brains for stupidity; to tear open his chest and pluck out his disloyal heart; and to blacken his eyes for his cowardice. In short, he would have torn Johnny to pieces small enough to thread a needle if Johnny had not been his best friend and most active supporter. In essence, he meant that if anyone else should even speak a word before he offered his own program, Fox would personally block up that passage with that boy's teeth. And the boys believed he could do it. They had seen him floor Fatty Mullins, touted as one of the toughest guys in St. Christopher. And though Fox was not as strong as their own Arty Lucas, and not as quick and agile as Johnny, they all knew he had the combination of their traits to beat them all "any day in the week and twice on Sundays."

Everyone listened to Fox with fear and wonderment as he told them what they would do and why. And when he finished they all agreed that nothing could be better. The fun would continue in a different way. Now they would all be deceivers carrying out an excellent plot through deception, preparing for the moment when Fox would give the secret signal. The signal was "Hey you guys, let's make Henry a member of our club."

"See, the idea's to treat 'em good and that way make the hurt worser," Johnny explained as their meeting ended.

So under Fox's scheme the tease continued; and it was fun for the boys again. Henry was not elbowed in the dining hall anymore. His food stayed on his plate until he himself had eaten it. To avoid arousing his suspicious nature, Alden was nudged a little still, and pinched. None of his food was taken. But seldom had his plate suffered an attack before. For as quickly as he could sit and get his hands on the shakers, he put his food, including desserts, out of sight with salt and pepper. Only sometimes, in retaliation for this evil deed, his food had been thrown under the table—a disposal best probably for Alden.

He ate as much as usual but he did lose some of his dumpiness as a result of running to school with the other boys instead of moping behind as he and Henry had done before.

With this new recognition Henry was happier. At first Alden was a little suspicious and reluctant but with Henry's constant pleading he joined in. Because of Alden's reluctance, accepting him into their scheme was easier than accepting Henry. Henry was so enthusiastic.

Fox and the others had agreed to meet after school to talk over the developing scheme. They met in the gym, a guard at the door to stop Henry and Alden should they appear.

"I told Henry about our club and he really swallowed it," Arty Lucas said.

Fox, jamming his head back with his hand, gave out a sound like the hissing of a snake as a muzzled dog might make it. "Oh, no! You gave it all away."

Of course no one knew why this was true but everyone agreed by united mumblings of distress. Fox stomped around with his head back and his hands up until Arty finally got up enough nerve to ask what had been wrong in that.

"What wrong? What wrong, he asks!" Arty was put back again and Fox continued to storm until Arty had been so stirred that he would either get up and leave in a rage or take a swing at Fox. Then Fox completely changed. He smiled.

"Arty, that's all right. We can fix it up. Just let me think a minute." And he went through all the motions of thinking.

"Aha! What we'll do is spread it; tell them all about our club."

"But we ain't got no club," Johnny interjected.

"Heck!" We've got a club! What's this? See, we can fit this right in with the initiation we'll give them."

A lengthy discussion of this new idea, "the initiation," followed, and then Arty mentioned he was getting to like Henry because he was such a good sport and always admired everything Arty said. Fox added that little Henry idolized Arty--Henry, though the same age as all, except Fox and Alden, who were older, was smaller than all except Billy Panda, who was no bigger than most of the boys in St. Andrew's-- but he idolized Fox and Johnny too, indicating that this was no reason to halt the development of the scheme.

Even Billy Panda rose and said that though he liked Henry very much the scheme must include him because he was Alden's buddy.

Why did Billy rise now and speak when he never had dared to do so before? If one did not know that Billy resented his size, or that he disliked everyone in Bartholomew, Christopher and all the higher dorms because they were potential tormentors, or that Billy Panda was a "holy horror" to a few of the smallest and weakest boys in St. Andrews, and, particularly, if one did not know that Billy hated only his potential tormentors and yet respected them only, one might surmise that Billy was applying a very good and necessary philosophical position to a practical problem.

As for Fox's outburst, if he were not so young it might be explained as the method of a very clever leader to keep tough Arty Lucas under his control. But this would be ascribing to this young boy a sense of drama, timing and eloquence which such a boy is not likely to possess—qualities, in addition to his strength, for which the other boys so admired Fox.

As for the entire group, it is like boys to do one thing which is wholly inconsistent with what they believe without giving a thought to the inconsistency—if they are even aware of it. Certainly this is the only explanation, other than Fox, for the boys' continuing their scheme against Henry in spite of their liking him.

Thus their meeting ended with an affirmation of the "club's" single aim: "to initiate 'em good," as Johnny put it.

Several days later, just after a game of "keep away" in the dorm, Fox thought he saw their new housemother in the hall about to make her accustomed leap into the dorm. On his signal everyone ran through the locker room into the bathroom and, one by one, they all climbed onto the fire escape and down to the ground.

"Come on," Johnny called to the three stragglers. He then ducked into the bathroom to make his own escape.

Alden and Billy Panda remained: Billy because he was too small and too weak to climb through the window; Alden because he hadn't an ounce of pluck in him. Henry followed as quickly as he could after retrieving his shoe, but not before Miss Grosvenor had burst through Bartholomew's door.

Miss Grosvenor had made escape through the bathroom window necessary because she had prohibited the playing of any games in the dormitory and she had sealed up the fire door the day before. She had other improvements in mind, but the means of accomplishing them eluded her. She believed in strict discipline, but had not so far been able to get control of the boys. Alden was an ally; and at first she regarded this as a major victory. For according to the jumble of records which she had studied carefully from the first, he was the oldest; and in her philosophy, the oldest influenced. Alden, on the other hand, expected nothing more than what he saw in Miss Grosvenor, a tall, slender, grey haired, and crisply starched ally and protector of all "to scale" airplanes, boats, and tanks.

But if the new housemother had been disappointed with Alden, she was surprised by her discovery about Henry, for in a very short time it had become apparent to her that he was at the center of everything, the chief trouble-maker. So if the boys had a scheme with Henry at its core she did too: subduing them through his subjugation.

In a week's time Miss Grosvenor had become quite convinced that Henry was the chief obstacle to her order and discipline. Billy had contributed to this conviction in exchange for her companionship. He would have preferred Miss Cunningham because her skirts were more abundant and he had not had to bargain for it with counterfeit confidence.

She was more convinced now than ever. She had distinctly heard Henry warn the others and direct them through the window, remaining until the last himself, as if to say "Catch me if you can!" Billy confirmed her belief even though Fox had given the signal and Henry had been the last to leave only because he had seen no compelling reason for or against running and because of that shoe.

But he did have a reason for wanting to run when she ushered him into the linen closet after his return from school. The closet was very small and the measuring stick in her hand very large. She said something about some records being in disorder and incomplete so that she would not know who or what was what for a while yet, but Henry was more interested in following that rule than her conversation.

"Mrs. Cunningham put three of your new shirts in Johnny's bin." Henry was only too happy to hear that he had so helped Johnny and he would have said so if that rule had not been so ominously twitched at that very instant.

"Did you see this closet before I came? No? Well it was in quite a disorder, let me say." Her face tightened. She squirmed just as if she were sitting on a pin cushion.

"Quite a disorder," she added as reflectively as someone sitting on pins and needles could be expected to add. "Just like the boys. And it's not like them at all. I know. Quite a disorder. And it is not like you at all, I know, to run up and down the halls; and in the dormitory with your games. It is not like you at all, is it? You are a young gentleman, you know, and you should make an effort to act like one; and set the example for the other boys instead of leading them into wrong ways, shouldn't you?

Henry might have remembered that not so long ago his attempt to explain the simplest thing to a more receptive soul had resulted in a most regrettably embarrassing moment. But Henry's shuddering was not from remembrance of things past. It was because of that measuring stick and the light—that bare, burning bulb still swaying hypnotically overhead, those beams caught by her glasses and cast into his eyes at a painful speed and blinding him each time she writhed in her chair. And what she said was like that light. He could see it but he could not grasp it. He knew that she disapproved of what he and the others had been doing but he could not understand why. He was deeply sorry that she was disappointed in them. He wanted to assure her that he would abandon his wrong ways, but he also had to add that she was wrong about his leading the others into wrong ways. He did not know which were the wrong ways, he said; and besides none of them which were the wrong ways. And besides, they all trusted Fox to lead them because Fox knew best. No, no one paid attention to Alden because he was not their leader because Fox was, and Fox always got them to go the right way which she might have thought they knew was the wrong way but which they did not know was the wrong way because they did not know which was the right way which they had thought the wrong way was.

Had he remained silent he might have suffered the same consequences, but it is a fact that Miss Grosvenor did not like mockery and whenever she encountered it she became very angry. But passing the blame, especially when the facts she had gathered proved the case, made her furious.

"In that case," she said, squirming and biting her lips as she reached for her measuring stick. Blinded by the searing light, his skull pricked by a thousand needles as the blood rushed to his head, Henry, horrified before he knew why he should be, was thrust over her lap and into a position to receive his first spanking.

Henry said nothing about the spanking when the other boys asked. He tried to avoid thinking about it because he knew that tears would come again, and tears, he thought, would wash away the foundation of friendship which he had been so long in building. As a result his answers were evasive, his manner furtive, very suspicious.

That evening as the boys were getting into bed Miss Grosvenor placed a list of do's and don'ts on the table before her.

"Gentlemen," she began, "today has been quite a disorder; and that is not as it should be. And that is not as it is going to be because each of you is going to mend his wrong ways, and each of you is going to act like a gentleman.

"Now I have been here more than a week. In that time I have seen many unmended ways. But now it is time to mend them. First, this afternoon there was a little misunderstanding about the use of the fire escape. Under no circumstances will it be used. Furthermore, I will not have any playing of games in the dormitory. It is a disgrace to our hallowed saint. There is no excuse for it with a gymnasium next door and the warm weather coming on."

The other don'ts were exhausted in another fifteen minutes. Then, having breezed through the dos, she looked up and saw all those young, attentive eyes down both sides of the dorm except:

"Arthur Lucas!"

"He fell asleep, Ma'am."

All those young eyes attended as she walked crisply down the aisle, stick switching with each stride.

"Mr. Lucas!"

She shook him.

He turned and bolted upright.

"The question, sir, is whether you are a gentleman." So intent was she upon a reply that she did not hear the muffled giggles when Arthur, apparently not yet awake, sank back onto his pillow.

"Mr. Lucas!" She shook him again.

He was finally awake. But her repeated question bewildered him. He scratched his head, toyed with his pajama buttons and after many facial contortions indicative of intense meditation, concluded that he probably was not a gentleman. Miss Grosvenor, who thought the goal of every living male thing was to be a gentleman, suffered an extreme shift in her pin cushion. She and the boy were too busy worrying each other like two mad dogs to hear the muffled laughter.

"Well you ought to be, don't you think? And if you ought to be, you ought to try to be, and if that is so, you ought to listen when you are being addressed—especially when a lady is addressing you for your own improvement. And you ought not to fall asleep as you did."

Though Arthur tried, he could not hold back the yawn that broke the static countenance of the situation. Charles Fox led in the laughter. Miss Grosvenor threw Arty on his stomach, and with a flick of her wrist, pulled down his pajamas. The measuring stick was applied. The laughing grew louder as the sound of the stick on bare flesh increased, especially as the housemother's face became more pained and Arty's more complacent.

Immediately when she turned the laughing stopped. Arty looked up as if he expected more.

"There, Mister. That ought to keep your attention for a while. If I hear a peep out of anyone else he will get the same. The behavior until now has been less certainly than it ought to be."

She resumed her seat and the boys went to their knees as she said the prayer. They crawled into bed again and she turned out the lights. The door swung shut on a cadent "Good night, Miss Grosvenor," but an airy "Good night, boys" hung in the room like a shroud for five minutes. And then someone asked Arty how he felt.

"Arty didn't even flinch," another whispered.

" 'Cause she can't swat, that's why," Johnny replied.

"Like to see you take it," Arty said.

"Fox could," Billy whispered.

"Why didn't you fight back?" Alden's voice was loud.

" 'Cause he don't want Father Solomon down on 'im, that's why."

"Fox is the only guy who could stand up to Father Solomon, huh Fox?"

"I don't hit ladies either," Fox replied, thus giving Arty nobility. "You did the right thing, Arty."

So with Fox's approval, Arty became the hero of the night. The boys admired Fox even more.

To combat the housemother's new program of gentlemanliness, Fox offered his scheme of deception at a meeting in the gym. They also discussed Henry. Miss Grosvenor had mentioned some things that she could not possibly have known unless she had been told. They all knew that Henry had gone in to see her after she had caught him at the fire escape. Unless he had snitched on them he would have been spanked. They knew that much about their new housemother. Henry had not mentioned being spanked. After questioning by Fox, Billy Panda swore that he saw no marks on Henry last night in the shower. Others tried to remember and then agreed with Billy. Henry had snitched!

And the best way to handle a snitcher was to involve him in everything that they did so he couldn't snitch on them without snitching on himself or without lying, and they all believed that, above all. God punished liars.

"Don't ever let a false word come from your lips," Father Solomon had said more than once, "for lying lips are abomination to the Lord; they that deal truly are His delight."

Not knowing the difference between right and wrong, Henry became a model for Miss Grosvenor's concept of a young gentleman. Consequently, he was very reluctant two days later when the old "keep away" circle was formed around him.

"We'll all get into trouble," he kept repeating as he tried to preserve them all from ungentlemanliness by retrieving the "Beaut: which they had wrested from Alden. With Henry to oppose, the game was fun again. It was getting faster and noisier. Then Fox stopped it by his little speech.

"How long have you been here, Hank?" he asked. Henry's new name surprised him. His father's name had been Hank. Being called Hank gave him a sense of accomplishment. At last the embarrassing scene could be forgotten. He liked it. "Hank!"

"Month and three weeks," Arty said quickly and draped his arm across Henry's shoulder.

Tears came to Henry's eyes despite his effort to control them. He loved them all.

"Do you fellows know what I'm just about to ask Hank?"

"No!" They all volleyed as if in rehearsed chorus. They closed the circle around him. Having conquered his tears, Henry beamed now instead.

"Henry, I mean Hank, do you want to be initiated into our club?"

Henry beamed even more and shook his head.

"Hey you guys, let's make Hank a member of our club." Fox gave it all the inflection that he might a new and spontaneous idea.

"To our den with him, men!"

Arty and Johnny grabbed him roughly, and the whole crowd followed with Fox farthest behind. They rushed through the door, Henry flushed with smiling and happiness. But had they gone any further they would have knocked over Miss Grosvenor for she had heard the noise and had rushed to discover the offenders on the path of wrong ways. She ushered them all right back into the dorm. She had looked through the peep-hole in the door soon enough to catch Henry leading the boys.

"Well, Mister," she said, "you cannot pass the blame this time, can you? So the first time was not enough, was it, Mister? Well you will no longer persist in your wrong ways. You will not be a bad influence on my boys."

His left ear was the means by which she dragged him through the dorm to her little desk where she kept her heaviest ruler. The other boys crowded around amazed, but not as amazed as Henry.

"Trousers down!"

Henry fought tears. This was to be his initiation, he knew. He tried to concentrate on something that would bolster him. His mother! That only made it worse. "Hank!" He focused his mind on "Hank!" He wavered; but only between pure bravery and abject defiance—a frequency to which he had never been attuned before.

"Trousers to the floor and quickly," she repeated. "The longer you wait the worse it will be!"

Henry flaunted time before her.

Miss Grosvenor was counting on a repeat performance to make up for her defeat by Arty. Breaking their leader before them would break the boys' desire for mischief.

Trousers down, he bent at the waist. With each whack his squinting eyes widened. Between each whack he filled with new hatred, stronger hate. She swung until she could swing no more and her arm fell limp.

Though his lips bled from biting, Henry had taken his paddling without a tear.

"Well, you didn't cry this time. But if there is a next time, believe me, you will. Now go wash your mouth out." She was too exhausted even to care about his bloody mouth. He too did not care.

Henry's blood had stunned as well as stultified the others, including Fox.

"What are the rest of you waiting for?" she blurted. "On your way before I take a stick to you too!"

Thereafter no one again thought of torturing Henry. He was really Hank to them now. They decided that the paddling had been initiation enough; and just to make Henry's membership in their club meaningful, they formed one—the "Bartholomew Bearcats." They now dedicated themselves solely to defying Miss Grosvenor by deception.

At first deception meant violating Miss Grosvenor's rules. Soon it meant doing everything behind her back that they considered bad. They had frequent fights with Andrews and Christopher. They sneaked away to the candy store across Lawrence Avenue. They roamed the neighborhood like a gang after school. Hank even joined. They swore as much as they could, including Hank who did not know what half the words meant. Hank even joined with the others in teasing Alden.

On their way to scout meeting Friday night they threw gravel at the picture windows in some new homes. When Alden threatened to go back and tell, Fox punched him in the belly. Billy hit him too. Alden began to cry and swing wildly at him. But Fox and Johnny and then Hank and Arty held him so he would not run.

As they were about to cross the street, a car stopped them. A woman got out and asked nervously if they had thrown any stones. They could see a man in the car. Fox stepped forward just as Alden started a scream—cut short as Hank's hand clamped down violently on his mouth. Arty jabbed his fist into Alden's belly to knock out the wind. They held him up as he writhed in their grip. The other boys closed in immediately so the woman would not see him.

"We're on our way to scout meeting, ma'am," Fox intoned in a manner not anyone would expect from a boy his age. "But a whole pack of guys tried to pick a fight with us just a few minutes ago. They hurt poor Alden here."

The ranks separated and Alden was revealed. The ranks closed.

"He'll be okay though; soon as we get him to the scoutmaster. Those boys went down that street."

The woman turned to the man in the car. "It was some other boys, George. They went down Mozart."

She turned to Fox. "Do you want us to follow you so there won't be any more trouble?"

"Oh that won't be necessary, ma'am," Fox replied. "We were in small groups before. There were only ten of them. Thank you anyway, ma'am."

When the car had pulled away, they walked on, laughing.

Miss Grosvenor never heard about the stones, but she did learn that Arty Lucas had hurt Alden. Alden had not told on Hank. He had not wanted to tell on Arty because of Fox's threats. But because he was sent to the infirmary he had had to tell on someone. Hank had not been included because Alden remembered how Hank had tried to save the "Beaut" from destruction several days before; the "Beaut being that time the newly finished "to scale model" German tank. Through this kindness Alden hoped to win back Henry's friendship. This, even though Henry must have caused the puffy red upper lip, and Arty, Fox and Billy only the less painful sore belly.

So only Arty was punished, but not in the usual way. Miss Grosvenor had suffered too many defeats at paddling. Arty was assigned to mopping the bathroom and locker room floors every night for a week after the others were in bed.

She connived to get Alden to confess that Hank was at the bottom of the fight but Alden would confess nothing. In lieu, she satisfied herself by alluding to her suspicion of Henry at every chance.

At first Miss Grosvenor's belief that Henry was the leader of Bartholomew had not affected Fox. It had been an advantage; and a great deception too. But these allusions gnawed at his pride. If he was the leader he certainly wanted to be recognized as such. Something had to be done to gain recognition from her even if it meant a paddling.

Her belief bothered the Panda too. After all, Henry was barely bigger than he! But what could he do? Henry could beat him in a fight. None of the others could be persuaded to gang up on him, especially by the Panda.

Paddlings were out now that Henry was like Arty.

That Wednesday after the all-school movie in the rumpus room, Billy poked his head into the Bartholomew locker room just long enough to see Johnny handing Hank a cigarette.

"Come on, Hank," he said. "It ain't bad fer ya. Jus' one puff!" Arty had already taken a puff. "It ain't gonna kill ya. Come on!"

Hank took a puff and then another.

Billy walked away when he saw Fox enter the dorm, nodded and then disappeared into the corridor.

Fox went into the locker room. There was smoke but no cigarettes.

"You didn't start a fire? With the fire escape sealed off and the window nailed shut?"

When Johnny saw it was only Fox, he offered him a cigarette. Arty and Hank pulled theirs out from under the lockers, brushed off the dirt and stuck them between their lips. Fox refused.

"I suppose you have a pack of your own in your locker, Hank?"

"Naw," said Johnny, "but you kin have this one if ya want. I already got a empty, and so's Arty, for ol' time's sake."

Henry was grateful. Having this empty pack in his locker gave him of sense of kinship with the others.

The next day Henry was accused of smoking. Someone had snitched on him, but not on Johnny or Arty. He would never tell on them because being a Snitcher On Buddies was almost as bad as being a liar. He confessed to Miss Grosvenor and received the same punishment she had given Arty.

Why he had been singled out puzzled him unless... All day he had fought down the only real explanation: Fox had snitched on him; but then why not on Arty and Johnny too? They both told him that Fox had not snitched because Fox would not do that. But they could give no other explanation.

At nine-thirty, when all the others were in bed, Henry was swishing the mop across the bathroom floor. It did not bother him. The odor of disinfectant was good. It cleared his head.

Fox sneaked in.

"Guess you got caught," he whispered. He smiled. "That will teach you to do things on your own without me."

Henry looked up from the floor and saw Fox smiling. It was clear now. Fox had been jealous. Fox had been jealous because of Miss Grosvenor; because she had always thought—and still did think—that Henry was the leader of the Bartholomew Bearcats.

"You snitched," he said, a little afraid.

"Me? I don't snitch and I don't lie. Those are the two things I don't do."

"You lied that night when the lady stopped us."

"That wasn't lying. That was getting us off the hook, all of us. That's different."

"Well, you snitched on me and that wasn't for all of us."

"I didn't snitch."

"No one else saw us." Henry was not whispering.

"Arty and Johnny saw you and…"

"Yeah, but they're my buddies. They wouldn't snitch."

"What about me, I'm your buddy too? Billy Panda saw you! Did you know that? I saw him sneaking away as I came in, I just remember. He must have snitched."

In Henry's mind Fox had just done something worse than lie and from that moment he was not the old Fox who would admit and fight. Henry had no more fear of him—or respect.

"That's a lie!" he shouted.

"Quiet, stupe," Fox whispered.

"That's a lie for yourself!"

Henry did not know quite how to act when angry. This was really the first time. He was disgusted but he could not express it—except in Fox's own words, the words Fox used when he was angry.

"You Stupe! Traitor! SOB! Liar! You're a snitcher and a lying traitor!"

"You take that back!" Fox shouted. "Take it back!"

"No!"

When Miss Grosvenor came in she brought all of Bartholomew with her. Henry was slumped on the wet floor holding his stomach with Fox over him, kicking.

"You stop that right now!" Miss Grosvenor shrieked. "Why this is the worst disorder I've seen! This oughtn't to be and you'll be sorry," Mister Fox. Why the idea!" She started to grab him but he boxed her hand away.

"Keep your hands off me!"

There was a pause of a minute in which only Henry's sobs could be heard.

"What do you mean by this?" She reached for him again and he boxed her hand away.

"You can do what you like with the others, but keep your hands off me!"

"This isn't like you at all, Charles; not like you at all. Now come to your senses. Now come along!" She reached for him again and this time overreached. Her flashing glasses fell to the floor.

"All right! All right, Mr. Fox," she screamed. "Since you have just proven you are not a gentleman, someone get Father Solomon."

"No one move!" Fox yelled.

"He's somewhere in the building. Someone go!"

"I'll go, Miss Grosvenor," Arty yelled, tears running down his cheeks. In fact all the boys were very shaken.

"Lucas, stay where you are," Fox bellowed.

Arty started off. Fox grabbed him by the back of the neck, but Johnny and several others tore him away.

They all joined in to hold Fox, while Miss Grosvenor groped for her glasses and kept screaming "Someone get Father Solomon. He's in the building." Arty ran out!

In a few seconds Father Solomon was in the Bartholomew bathroom.

"All right boys. All of you back to bed," he said. "You too Charles. We'll discuss it in the morning.

"Yes, Father."

Then Father Solomon took Henry and Miss Grosvenor to the infirmary. Henry had only a little wind to gain back. Miss Grosvenor had a cut across the bridge of her nose. It was the only thing she could see without her glasses.

Henry went in to see Alden. Having slept most of the day, he was still awake. Henry apologized and they shook hands. Henry said he could be a member of their secret club if they still had one when he came back.

Miss Grosvenor came in and hugged them both. They would have a club, she said, and it would be called the "Do-Gooders." Henry did not want any clubs, and he did not want them because if there were clubs there would always be outcasts like Alden and he didn't want outcasts like Alden because Alden was okay as he was even if he did look like an olive with his red lip. And Henry was so happy. At last he had expressed what he meant and felt at the same time; and someone understood.

But Miss Grosvenor was set on the "Do-Gooders." She was even more convinced that it would work now that Fox had moved on to Christopher. Father Solomon had given him a good beating. The rumor was that even the indomitable Fox had shed some tears this time.

Henry did not want the "Do-Gooders," but Miss Grosvenor made him the first member and President. Each week one more member was to be added unless there were none worthy. She bought games and puzzles which only the "Do-Gooders" could use.

Henry disliked her just as much as he had before and just as much as he had learned to dislike Fox, but he went along with her scheme because he had learned what was right and what was wrong in her eyes. He knew too that nothing he had ever done was either right or wrong and that whatever he was likely to do in the future would not be right or wrong. He had learned to go the right way for Miss Grosvenor without going the wrong way for Arty and Johnny and all the others, even Billy. The "Do-Gooders" had no more advantages or secrets than anyone else. Behind Miss Grosvenor's back Henry let everyone play with the games and puzzles. Sometimes they played "keep away" in the dorm just for fun too.

Miss Grosvenor was happy. All the boys were happy. And Henry was happy. That was right. Goodness for Henry was knowing how to make other people happy, not a strict old set of rules or childish innocence. Miss Grosvenor's gentlemanliness was part of it and Fox's deceit was too.

➢

FALL

(A Christmas Story)

By George Hook

I

This was the first of the ten hour days for Robert Smith's. The sales personnel, in their traditional dark blue, were hurrying to their posts behind the counters after the final pep assembly of the morning. All was quiet for a moment as they went through the procedure of checking out their counters. The managers, three on each floor, waited for their sections to finish and then started on their checking tour. There was a stream of whispering, a breaking off into silence and then a single sound of opening cash registers—the time-perfected unison in which each member of the staff took pride each morning before opening.

Silence reigned as all stood anxiously waiting. The tree, the largest in the entire city, stretched magnifi-

1

cently from its snow-like dais to within a few feet of the fifth floor. It was ornamented with glistening silver balls which changed from red to blue to green and other colors depending on the rotation of the vari-colored lights from above. Light-colored streamers extended to the tree from the balustrades of the four white marble walls of each of the seven floors. The first floor was rearranged in the traditional Christmas fashion. Children's toys were on display under the tree. There was a vast network of tracking, a huge outlay for electric trains and equipment. The nearby counters were laden with other toys and children's gifts. The outlying counters displayed fit items for men and women; the two sections separated by the tree and surrounding toys. Here is where items from the various sections throughout the store were prominently displayed.

Shortly after nine, two uniformed men walked ceremoniously down the red carpeted aisles toward the great glass-paneled revolving

2

doors to set them free. Red-faced customers jammed the aisles, bringing with the fresh brisk outside air into the fir scented warmth of the vast halls.

Megie, who had been a part of Robert Smith's Christmas season for nearly twenty years, moved from one counter to another helping over-burdened sales girls and advising and directing customers. "Megie"—the name given by her fellow workers; an affectionate diminutive of that abominable other name which none of them could ever bring themselves to use—who was so charming and accommodating always during any other time, became an irritable and haggard old maid as soon as she was moved from the third floor for the Christmas season. It was either the terribly long hours or the bustling crowds which frenzied her, perhaps both, making her a menace after the first several hours. She had been the same every Christmas for the past few years. Some of her friends had suggested

3

that she be replaced during this time, or at least not moved from her normal post; but their suggestions were not heeded and there she remained. And each year a few more customers fell victim to her petty wrath. Each year she took away a measure of someone's seasonal spirit and joy.

Late in the morning, during a temporary lull in the store's activity one of the salesladies in Megie's section had motioned to her. Megie by this time was exhausted and cross; already several customers had touched off her fury. She needed some rest, some awakening experience or sight, sweet and curious to soothe her. The sales girl smiled pleasantly and pointed down the aisle.

"Look Megie! The little boy! Isn't that cute?"

Megie looked down the aisle. She saw; and shocked by what she saw, she stood fuming, growing red with anger and embarrassment. Her responsibility; it was her responsibility, she thought. As if there hadn't been enough already for one day.

"Don't you think that's cute, Megie? But maybe he's lost; you better see..."

She turned toward Megie just as she started briskly down the aisle. Megie went faster down the aisle crying, "You, you! What are you doing?" She was furious. "What are you doing, you?" she cried, spirited by her rage.

II

The snow had come during the night, covering the bare ground and trees, clothing in white the black which in Stephen's memory had been only a little while ago so green. Suzy had just gone in to get a kitchen pot from her mother to use as a helmet. Stephen had continued to mold out the snowman's body until Suzy was in; he rested, wiping his moist face with the backs of his gloves, and knelt to pack more snow into the bottom mound. It would be a tall snowman; Stephen imagined him a warrior, big, and proud and strong.

The snow was coming down, though not so much as during the night. It soon covered over all tracks in the yard, making it appear as if no one had ever either come or gone. Stephen pressed against the snow mound to protect his bare face from the wind and spraying snow. He looked down the block, watching a figure in the distance, dark against the snow. He watched the man pass and disappear. The street was now empty, and Stephen waited.

Stephen began working again when he saw Suzy coming out. He rolled a large snowball for the warrior's head and looked up only after Suzy spoke. He felt the warrior's helmet and nodded approval.

"I'll go home and get my sword now, okay?"

He maneuvered out to the sidewalk and traced the stranger's steps, which had come out of the distance, up the block toward his home, leaving them as they went beyond his walk. When he got to the porch he looked back and saw Suzy crowning their snowman. He stumbled up the stairs, reached up and rang the bell. The door opened and there was his mother looking down at him as he breathed in the pleasant warmth of their home. She knelt and, holding him as he stood motionless, she felt the coldness of his cheeks. She unzippered his snowsuit and threw back its furry hood

"My little Stephen feels cold? She whispered with a baby-like inflection.

Stephen shook his head. "Mommy," he blurted, "do you know where my sword is?"

She looked at him quizzically and, overcome by his love-commanding wide blue eyes and his delicate touch, she drew him gently near and caressed him, kissing his cold, moist face. His head resting against her cheek, he, sniffing the cleanness of her hair, felt an earthly warmth mingled with pleasant freshness—a tingle. He felt the little dot of coldness on his cheek, though, and as his mother moved away, loosing him from her gently swaying grip, he saw her earring—a small blue stone with a silver rim, getting smaller as she rose to her full height.

"Stephen, do you remember what Daddy told you was downtown?" she said as she put on her coat and galoshes.

Stephen remembered. Daddy had told him about the wreaths, the ribbons and banners, the sleighs and reindeer, the displays in store windows, about Santy Claus and his helpers. Some of the neighborhood kids didn't believe in Santy Claus. But he and Suzy did.

"Are we going to see Santy Claus, Mommy?"

"You saw Santa last year. You can't expect to see him every year, Stephen. You remember how long we had to wait last year, and how tired you got. You can write him a letter this year, Stephen. How would you like to do that? We'll go downtown and you can look at the toys. I'll help you write the letter, Stephen."

Stephen didn't want to write a letter. He couldn't understand why he should not see the Santy this year which his mother said he had seen last year but which he didn't remember seeing. He finally accepted his mother's reasoning as his own.

Stephen and his mother left the house. The snow was very lightly falling now, and Stephen looked to see that Suzy was gone. The helmet was there, reminding him of the sword. There were only the single prints of the stranger as they went downtown; otherwise the snow was new and difficult for Stephen to walk in.

Soon they were walking shoveled walks and looking into the windows of the outlying stores. They played the game of naming things: Stephen's mother asking "What's that" and pointing; Stephen replying in general terms.

They fell to silence. Stephen concentrated on keeping warm. They had walked for several blocks when Stephen asked, "Mommy, where's Daddy? Is he working again today?"

"Oh, look Stephen!" she said suddenly, pointing to the decorations along the streets. They were downtown. Around the corner and half-way up the block was the biggest department store in town. Stephen kept looking up and up, nearly stumbling as he tried to count the stories; but before he could he and his mother were through the revolving door of Robert Smith's.

III

Stephen's mother tightened her grip on his little hand; he enjoyed the warm close contact with the crowd as he trailed her through the aisles toward the tree, looked at the tree and breathed in the pleasant freshness of the clean fir scent. He stared, wide-eyed, at the glistening ornaments changing colors and silver. He took in the uniqueness of each ornament in the splendor of the whole, looking up until he could barely see them. Then his eyes steeled on the red and white striped candy canes which hung from the base.

His mother knelt beside him whispering to him: "Stephen, would you like a candy cane?" He felt the coldness against his cheek and nodded, looking suddenly into her face.

"I'll get you one before we leave. Remind me, Stephen," she said softly.

"You won't be afraid if I leave you here alone with all these toys, will you?" and she swept her arm across the scene of toys. Stephen shook his head in a manly, yet innocent way.

"Everything will be all right, Stephen, if you stay here and look at the toys. I'll be in the men's department over there only for about fifteen minutes, so there isn't anything to worry about."

She rose and went. With apprehension he watched her leaving; his eyes followed her. He looked again at the tree and then around at the toys which surrounded him. He leaned against the fence and watched the little blue and white diesel streak through a mountain tunnel with its train of freight cars. He noticed the detail of the mountains, the trees and streams, the mountain lodge and the town on the miniature plane before him. It was an entire world in miniature, lacking only in a sky of its own. Waiting for the diesel, he watched a slower, stronger black steam engine chug around and down the mountain.

The store was very crowded; others pushed around him. He struggled through them to look at the many shiny-red fire engines—the water trucks and hook-an-ladders. There were trucks and cars, cowboys and Indians, doctors, nurses, lawyers, soldiers; and roads and planes, hospitals and courthouses, torn up battlefields—a vast array in plastic. Stephen savored each scene and object; he was caught up in a flight of fancy. He would be a great soldier in a tight black uniform; big and strong and brave—a warrior flashing a golden sword which would catch the light of day glistening from Suzy's golden face as she stood on a hill against the sun. He would be a great doctor clothed in white; surrounded by pure whiteness, he would learn great secrets. Or he would be paid the reverence due a black-robed judge; the reverence he had seen his father paid in court.

Now Stephen was jostled by the crowd which seemed to swell in waves and then subside. He was caught up by the winding back-and-forth motion. Awakened suddenly, he felt dazed and helpless—a little boy among men. Frightened and lost, he strained to see, to get a glimpse of the tree and orient himself. It was no use; he was immersed, lost, blinded by the closeness and immediate height of the undulating crowd.

He wandered, not knowing where he was, frightened, and hoping to find his mother. And then, as always, there she was. He caught a glimpse of her; only a flash of her red woolen dress did he see. He desperately fought his way toward her. There it was again. He reached; grasping firmly to the dress, and escaped from the flowing aisle. Nothing happened. His mother didn't reach down and take his hand. He looked up and was shocked. The dress was red, wool, his mother's; this was his uncoated mother. But, the eyes, the face, all her features remained fixed. Her arms gestured meaninglessly. He took his hand from the only resemblance of his mother's warmth, the dress, and stood back into the emptying aisle, stricken. He stared up at the cold lifeless form, the statue of his mother.

He slowly came to his senses. Stephen had seen these before, but only from a distance. Never had he seen one so closely resembling his own mother. To see her face thus, so coldly portrayed, was terrifying. And yet, he felt only a sensation of emptiness. He stared at this thing. He stood and looked at her every feature, becoming more curious until, wondering if he could evoke warmth, the affection he had known, he reached out.

IV

Stephen heard the furious cry. It came to him muffled and from a great distance. He looked out from the woolen dress to see the frightening formless shape hovering over him. Impulsively, he ran. He ran down the aisle, up another, around a counter, past the stairs which led from the overlooking balcony. He ran past the elevators into a maze of bundled human shapes. He edged his way through, sapped of breath and strength. He heard her shouting "Stop him! Stop him!" He didn't dare to look back. He ran in search of his mother; but then, he was grasped, and arrested, halted, lifted from the floor by the black clothed arms which surrounded him. He was numbed, paralyzed as he was drawn toward the panting form.

Megie clawed at him and rasped: "Thank goodness! We've caught you!" And she whispered under her breath: "You little pervert."

Stephen burst into tears when he realized he was safely in his father's arms. And through his tear-stained eyes he saw her looking up at him.

"Give him to me!" she said. "I'll take him. Thank you, but I'll take him now. I'll take him from you now!"

Stephen's father, his chest heaving, commanded her away in a voice that halted the surrounding activity. Megie shrank from him and, looking around her at the crowd that had gathered, she raised her hands to her head and tore at her hair, crying into the dead silence: "Oh, what have I done! What am I doing! What have I done!"

One of the salesladies led her away, crying and mumbling. Stephen had stopped crying when his father had shouted out; and now he was trembling from excitement, fatigue, from an indefinable fear as he watched her leave.

Stephen and his father were surrounded by curious strangers. And then his mother broke through the crowd with the two other managers. She took little Stephen in her arms and caressed him as the managers made apologies to the father.

"Is there anything we can get your boy? Anything at all?" one of the managers asked, looking back and forth between the father and Stephen, whose head was resting on his mother's shoulder. Stephen's mother rested her head on his and pointed to the tree.

"One of those," she said. The one manager smiled while the other went to the tree and took from it a large candy cane. He brought it back and ceremoniously held it out to Stephen.

"Take it, Stephen," his mother said; and Stephen reached out and took it.

V

The streets were overflowing with cars. "We could walk home faster than this," Stephen's father said after several minutes of creeping along, still in the same block. Stephen had settled peacefully on the back seat of the car with his candy cane held tightly in his fist. His mother had looked back to see that he was asleep. She turned and asked: "What happened? What was it all about? Why was that woman screaming?"

"Oh, the whole thing was really rather silly," he said as he steered the car forward on the icy streets.

"He somehow got over into the wrong section. He was wandering around and then he stopped dead still in front of a dummy. What he did was really quite amusing; that that old woman—no doubt an old maid; she probably is—thought he was doing something indecent. As if a little boy like Stephen could do anything indecent! She started chasing him, threatening him. The woman must have been out of her mind! I ran down from the balcony as quickly as I could."

There was a long pause. He broke the silence: "It wasn't our fault. We had good intentions. Things like that are bound to happen. He was protected from her. He'll remember that! And he'll also remember that I was there when he needed me! He'll remember that I told her to get away and to keep her goddamned hands off my son!"

They crept home slowly while Stephen dreamed. He had returned with his golden sword to find the snowman almost completed. Suzy stood there shaping it. He had held his sword to her, poetically; and she had taken it. With it she began to etch the snowman's features. "No! No!" he cried as he lunged at her. She turned on him with the sword, waving it in the cold, snow-laden air. He stepped aside and grasped her wrist, cracking it over his knee. The sword was his! He swung at the warrior-snowman, lopping off its head. He watched head and helmet fall to the ground, rolling round, rolling, rolling round.

Stephen started. He awoke in dizziness. The car had stopped and his mother was carrying him into their home.

➢

SUGAR

By George Hook

I

As she sat in the offices of the
Drug Enforcement Agency ("DEA")—
Children's Flying Wing, Genevieve
Swag listened to the pre-raid activity.
She was there at the special invitation
of the Director of the Children's Flying
Wing as a reward for her article within the past year which had traced the
history leading to the Wing's creation.
Sad to say the article had been rejected for a Pulitzer as propaganda.
However, it had received the Reagan
for journalism most contributing to
the exposure or resolution of society's
problems. That award, though not as
prestigious as the Pulitzer, the Reagan, was ten times more rewarding
monetarily.

Gene's article, "Journey to the
Ultimate Solution," had explained the
government sponsored research, chem-

ical, psychological and sociological, which had led to the conclusion that the source of all addiction, most disease and societal dysfunction was sugar, that although one form, glucose, was essential to life, it was produced by the body from starch and hence all other forms were superfluous if not actually harmful. This had been good news for the carbohydrate crowd, the bread and pasta purveyors, and the insurance companies, which were permitted to increase premiums to cover the high risk of sugar consumption just as they had alcohol, tobacco and alternative life styles, in the past. Added to the natural disincentives of publicity, higher premiums and the resultant peer opprobrium, were government burdens and punishments, including registration and reporting requirements for manufacturers, distributors and consumers of sugar and their byproducts, punishments for unlawful manufacture, distribution, possession and consumption paralleling the drug prohibitions and penalties, the Food and Drug Administration ("FDA") having declared it and its precursors (sugar cane, honey, fruits, malt and milk), and derivatives (pastries, pies, cakes, candies) drugs and the Attorney General having placed them under Schedule II with those other scourges of society:

alcohol (C_2H_6O), caffeine ($C_8H_{10}N_4O_2$), cannabis sativa ($C_{18}H_{24}O_2$), cocaine ($C_{11}H_6NO_2$), epinephrine ($C_9H_{13}NO_3$), ephedrine ($C_{10}H_{15}NO$), estrogen ($C_{18}H_{24}O_2$), heroin ($C_{21}H_{23}NO_5HCl$), lysergic acid ($C_{16}H_{16}N_2O_2$), methamphetamine ($C_6H_6CH_2CH(NHCH_3)CH_3$), morphine ($C_{17}H_{19}NO_3$), nicotine ($C_{10}H_{14}N_2$), steroids and testosterone ($C_{19}H_{28}O_2$).

Obviously, this had been bad news for the sugar cane countries-- India, Peru, Brazil, Bolivia, Colombia, Australia, Ecuador, Cuba, Philippines, El Salvador, even Hawaii--and fruit growers initially. They had been forced to accept a pittance upon condemnation of their crops or destruction by defoliants and, if they were lucky, fire, which did not deactivate their fields for years. The United States had muscled this result with threats of cutting off all aid and crop subsidies for a decade otherwise. Unnecessary to state was the possibility of pre-emptive strike by the United States to effect regime change of those who defied US Policy.

Officially, there had been 100% compliance. Actually, as with alcohol, initially during Prohibition, from 1920 through 1933, which encouraged the drink soaked Roarin' Twenties and enriched the Mafia beyond measure, as with cocaine and marijuana, initially as Nixon's retributions for the opposition and disrespect of youth, and especially Blacks, for him and his policies, which had the same effect as Prohibition of shifting the source from responsible doctors and pharmacists, to the irresponsible, those too unqualified or too impatient for regulated, legal enterprise, as with tobacco, which was wrenched from the bankrupted traditional farmers, manufacturers and quaint tobacconists and liquor and grocery store and restaurant retailers, a vast, shadowy net work of illicit cane was grown domestically, imported surreptitiously, and converted into pure and confectioners sugar, and from their sold to ultimate users or delivered to what became known as bake houses. As with alcohol, drugs and tobacco, many of those who had theretofore engaged in the legitimate business, went bankrupt when the prohibitions were adopted. Many of these resumed their occupations on the other side of the law in order to support themselves and their families, aligning themselves, at an exorbitant cost, with those who would protect them from government interception, destruction, prosecution and prison. As with alcohol, drugs and tobacco, the government revenues from legitimate business plummeted as it fed into illicit shadows. As with these, the enforcement cost—investigation, interdiction, incarceration—had soared. Taxation of legitimate enterprise and incomes had to increase substantially, despite the large forfeitures of business and personal estates, including bank accounts, vehicles and bake houses engaged in the "sinister sugar trade."

The government had anticipated that there would be some dislocation in food production and distribution and created a vast regulatory scheme to alleviate, if not entirely eliminate it, hiring from among those whose jobs in the sugar trade had been eliminated by its legislated prohibition. Primarily, the regulation sought to eliminate hoarding, the innate primitive response to stress and scarcity, by imposing quotas on food acquisition, possession and consumption. Unfortunately, the government had been dilatory in setting up the food bureaucracy and it had spent longer than expected in drafting and finalizing the regulations. Once they were in place and the regulators deputized, there was substantial delay and error in allocating and issuing food quota stamps, many of which were then stolen from the mails and sold at exorbitant prices in black markets throughout the Nation and in every community.

During the period of implementation crops rotted or went to seed, many of the legitimate food businesses and farmers went bankrupt, a general famine ensued and the economy went into depression. There was an epidemic of farm, grocery, train, truck and warehouse burglaries and robberies. There were many deaths in self-defense, as well as summary executions and life prison sentences to set examples. In sum, however, the honest law abiding citizen starved and died or suffered loss of living and property. All others, being the great majority, adapted to the new society restrictions and cheated and stole to survive and, in a few cases, prosper.

As the governmental officials, including the politicians in D.C. and the media were largely immune from these vicissitudes, having priority and exemption as well as access to the numerous extra-legal and illegal sources of production and distribution, none of the Drug Enforcement people, nor Genevieve Swag had any realization of, or sympathy for, the general suffering. They focused on the ultimate good of the government initiative and to the extent they perceived any pain, they believed it to be a necessary predicate to achieve the ultimate good—which was to eliminate all addiction, disease and societal dysfunction.

However, the Reagan award had been made primarily because of Gene Swag's laudatory history of saving the children, "More than a Million Saved" at the publication date of "Journey to the Ultimate Solutions." She was now to be favored with a specific child saving operation. Meticulously honest reporter that she was, Gene had insisted that she be permitted to drop in on an operation unannounced within the week designated so that she could see a real operation unaffected by the anticipation of her presence. This, however, had been rejected by the Director as impractical because of personnel allocations and also because she would have to be deputized as *posse comitatus,* and actually perform Flying Wing tasks to avoid strict rules against the press accompanying the police on raids which had evolved after the Supreme Court case which had resulted in the award of substantial damages for evasion of privacy therefor.

II

Accordingly, Gene had appeared just before the Commissioner departed. She was deputized, receiving an appropriate deputization certificate. She had been briefed on her duties. She was to carry a camera and record the raid. She now sat in the control room waiting.

The confidential informant's phone rang. The control room operator flipped the switch. The speaker and recorder were on.

"Hello, this is LaFarge, reporting a happenstance while on cruise off-duty. About 1500 hours, observed nubile female with empty grocery bag heading in direction of known speakeasy bake house. Waited 15 minutes before she emerged with full bag. Followed to walk-up on Lakeview. Positioned myself to observe unobserved. Waited."

The report was slow as stitching, so annoying in its formality.

"Why does she talk that way?" Gene asked, whispering.

"Shh," the Director admonished as to a child, and then thinking better of it, responded. "Hold, one moment LaFarge. She's voice communicating to the computer here," pointing, "which will prepare and sign her report and convert it to an affidavit should it be needed for a warrant for arrest or search. Anything else before we resume?"

"Yes. Is her name LAFARGE?"

"Her pseudonym. She's an undercover confidential informant. No name. Never disclosed. She never appears."

"The Courts let you get away with that?"

"Yes, on assurance she's a reliable source. Ready? Resume, La-Farge!"

"Made store check readout request."

Gene's hand sprang up, duly admonished not to interrupt verbally. The Director ignored it.

"A child with book pack rushed up the stairs and into the home, followed shortly by five other children, all boys, same age, dropped off by their mothers with overnight bags, bearing presents.

"Store check read out received. Entire purchases consisted of contraband: sugar, coffee, milk, ready made frosting, whipped cream, cake, chocolate chip cookies, ice cream, candies and assorted soft drinks. Field estimate: sugar content enough to knock each kid off the hyperactivity charts twice over. Young adult male, presumed father, just appeared. Moving on! Out!"

Gene was happy that a Friday night had been chosen for her. This sounded like a serious sugar bust in process. She could now have a glorious week-end developing the story and maybe get a good headline front page in the Monday edition as well as her byline column. She now relaxed, sat back in her chair, gathering herself for the next burst of activity. She watched as the control room computer spewed out the application for search and arrest warrants and affidavits, noted receipt by the Duty Magistrate, then automatically asked "any question?" "No," was the immediate response. A second later the warrants issued executed by the Magistrate.

III

The kids had finally settled down in their sleeping bags, as best the Flinches could expect after their son's seventh birthday party. John had just dozed off when he was awakened again by a faint knocking at the front door, he thought. It grew louder and insistent. He looked at the clock, one, and his wife, still asleep. She had worn herself out with the preparations and the party. Who could be at the front door at this hour? He put on his robe, shuffled into his slippers, scratched his head and went to the door, which suddenly came tumbling down upon him.

"Freeze, DEA," the first person through shouted, automatic in hand and brandishing. "Down on your knees, hands behind your back." Too startled to do anything else, he obeyed and was soon cuffed and shoved into a corner.

Patricia came running out half-naked, screaming when she saw John against the wall and the menacing group coming over the door, a burly armed male leading and five Furies following with Gene bringing up the rear as camera toting chronicler. The boys followed. She was grabbed, thrown onto the sofa and told to shut up. The boys were each grabbed, pricked with a needle, blood drawn, placed against a patch, and thrown onto a heap where they bawled without mercy. A white coated woman with a doctor's bag placed in front of her placed each patch in a separate plastic bag, infinitely more carefully than she had done the pricking, likewise stacking them in the same order as the boys.

"You," she said to the boy on top of the stack, "name and address." His bawling prevented answer until stopped by the brute, who bellowed a heart stopping, "answer now you little toad or I'll squish you good."

Each boy answered in turn as the one atop was pulled off and the nurse shouted "next!"

"Now," announced the brute, "Mrs., you have the right to refuse questioning, but not providing a blood sample, and I will have to give you the opportunity to consult with an attorney before you confess."

As no mother is afraid of her own blood, only her child's, which had already been extracted with the expected dual trauma, Patricia opted for the drawing of blood, 4ccs which would be preserved for laboratory testing. John would neither talk nor submit. Instead, he was shouting, "This is an outrage. You can't do this. You can't get away with this. I'll sue you from here to kingdom come. You're damn right I want to talk to my attorney."

Through it all, the brute held him down, not difficult, since John's hands were cuffed behind his back, and the nurse extracted a healthy dose of blood from a vein after a dry feint at his buttocks for punishment.

The others gathered the garbage, the contents of the refrigerator and cupboards and finally drained the toilet and its effluence from the basement for qualitative and quantitative chemical analysis.

In addition to Gene's camera, one of the others took snapshots of the parents, John and Patricia Flinch, now the accused, and children, now the victims, as the results were immediately fed back to the control room at headquarters where the necessary complaints and affidavits were already prepared for the probable cause and bail hearings that would occur after daylight came.

IV

A paddy wagon with Nazi-sounding sirens and lights flashing so as to wake and intimidate the entire neighborhood pulled up. John and Patricia were pushed into the back and taken to holding cells for court appearances. They would appear before the magistrate unbrushed, unbathed and unrepresented in prison orange that day. Within a short time they would be tried, found guilty and sentenced for manufacturing, possessing, distributing and using a controlled substance. They would also be convicted on contributing to the addiction, disease and dysfunction of five children. The sentence for the controlled substance, based on the amount was a statutory minimum of ten years. Since they were first time offenders, they could get a sentence below that, but the guideline dictated that they get more and the judge, whose son had been killed by heroin, gave them twenty years. The contribution charge mandated sterilization and a minimum five year sentence per child. Since Patricia had obtained the contraband, prepared it and served it to the children and also assisted her son in sending out the drug party invitations under the guise of a birthday party, she was deemed to be the "drug king pin" and received an additional sentence of ten years. Although, he was apparently a more passive participant, John had resisted blood sampling and in so doing had set a bad example for the children, constituting resisting the legitimate orders of a government enforcement official and obstruction of justice, including threats of retaliation. For this he was sentenced to an additional ten years. In consequence, both John and Patrician were sentenced to incarceration for 65 years. Also, their entire assets were criminally forfeited and directed to be paid over to the Fund to Save the Children. Neither saw each other again, nor their children.

V

Gene gave her camera to the Head of the Flying Wing and went with a matron and little Billy Flinch to the Youth Rehabilitation Center where he would be designated and remain, probably until majority, for treatment, and, if luck would have it, cure, assuming that the Fund to Save the Children and tax allocations would be sufficient throughout the period for that purpose.

The number of children to be saved was increasing exponentially each year.

The Center Superviser, Ms. Vice, no first names to be used at the Center, attempted without success to soothe Billy. It was not like the old days when a cookie and milk or hot chocolate might do the trick. Nothing was the order of the day, at most tofu, for which kids had to develop a taste. She put him in a crib in isolation and assigned an orderly to watch over him from the shadows. After Billy had cried himself to sleep, he awakened to see this dark person lurking in the shadow, his screaming unrequited as the confused orderly maintained his place, exhausting himself to sleep again. The cycle repeated several times before dawn.

VI

Ultimately, Billy acclimated to his plight. He recovered virtually immediately from whatever addiction, disease and dysfunction he had. However, there was no love in his life, no concern, no sympathy, no understanding. As soon as he was old enough and able, he escaped from the Center to lead a life as a heartless marauder. Before being shot by police and killed, what countless numbers of murders, robberies and thefts he had committed is unknown, not for addiction or disease, but for food and shelter and to be left alone.

VII

Many years after their initial encounter Genevieve Swag cited the case of Billy Flinch in her shorthand without naming him, as she had forgotten his name, if she'd ever known it, and as he had died without a name, not knowing it himself, as an example of the dysfunctional youth that could slip between the cracks and that could have been saved by Save the Children had they been discovered soon enough to lead productive lives as citizens pursuant to the course of discipline that Ms. Vice had explained to her that night when Billy had been put in her charge.

VIII

Gene worked all week-end. Her initial story was headlined in the Monday edition. She covered the separate trials of John and Patricia Flinch. For reduced sentences they agreed to testify that the other parents knew that their children were going to attend a "drug party," not merely an innocuous birthday party at which pasta and water were to be served. Based upon the instructions of the judge, the jury had no choice but to find each parent guilty, with the exception of one lucky father who had been away on a business trip at the time and was able to prove that he knew nothing about the party until after it was over. However, his wife had told him about it upon his return, late Friday night. He had been charged additionally with misprision of a felony for his failure to report his wife immediately. His attorney's motion to strike the indictment on the ground of spousal privilege, that is, the right of a spouse to prevent a spouse from testifying and not being compelled to do so, was denied by the judge. It applied solely to testimony in a judicial proceeding, he ruled. At their trial, the wife's confession was introduced. In it she stated that she had told her husband about the party, including the sugar and sugar products that the children were to consume. However, the judge had properly instructed the jury to take the confession solely as evidence against the wife and not the husband so that on appeal his conviction for the misprision was upheld, the jury having sufficient other evidence to convict, especially his efforts to hide his wife when the DEA finally came, which seemed perfectly natural for a husband to do and he would have done had he the opportunity. However, he hadn't, as his wife had been the one to answer the door. The DEA had lied at the urging of the Assistant US attorney, who subtly suggested the scenario in his probing of the agent and his assertion that otherwise there was no basis for the indictment.

The convictions were hailed by Gene in her "Save the Children" series as a great victory for the children. Save the one father, the parents were all sterilized and sentenced to 15 years in prison. He was shot and killed along with his wife, when he attempted at the conclusion of one visitation to rescue her from prison.

The boys who had gone to the party were committed to separate Youth Rehabilitation Centers. One of them committed suicide, two became petty thieves, made the mistake of moving to California, where upon stealing a $10 pizza and two bottles of sparkling water, they were arrested, their prior records discovered and sentenced to life in prison under California's three strikes law. Another became a hopeless drunk, despite the unavailability of legal booze, and spent the rest of his short life in a mental institution.

The fifth one, who, like his father was very bright, but undisciplined, unlike his father, confined his addiction to one marijuana cigarette, which he did not inhale, and his disability to unzipping at unfortunate times, became a successful schmoozer and politician.

Their other children, being orphaned, disappeared into obscurity with patronyms other than their own.

Genevieve Swag won another Reagan for her story, "The Children Saved." In it she described how the resources of the State had been employed to purify the food supply not only for the children but for all mankind, "for to the State we are all its Children."

IX

For her next story, she had been allowed to trace the supply of food from its origins on the prison farm co-operatives, where strict governmental supervision and inspection assured minimal sugar content, to the prison processing plants where the blocks of starch were formed and flavored, to the prison warehouses where the packages of food were stored subject to call by the Regional Commissioners against presentation of food quota stamps.

X

The food quota stamps had become a permanent fixture. They could be obtained upon application to the Federal Office of Food Quality Assurance ("FOQA"). Except for the extraordinary effort and the time waiting, they were free from that source. For the most part, however, they were only available on the black market at exorbitant prices, as administrative exhaustion, starvation, and market forces—which necessarily included bribing officialdom--compelled everyone to go to that uncertain source.

XI

And so, ultimately everyone lived healthily, if not happily, ever after.

THE END

CAPTURE THE FLAG

BY George Hook

I

When I was a kid, I went to camp summers. One summer we played this neat game called "Capture the Flag." Saboteurs were designated weeks ahead who were to start out beyond the perimeters designated and proceed to the flag pole in the center and at the lake's edge of the camp. The saboteurs did not know each other or how many. Each was to proceed from his own point and make his own way to the pole. Of course, this was a flag pole that flew the American Flag during the day. We were young, patriotic kids. So we would not actually capture the flag. Although we were called saboteurs, the pole would not be blown up or damaged. Although we had 4th of July fireworks on the lake, they would not be used either. The name was used just to lend mystery and intrigue to a kid's game.

Merriam came to me when I was alone and told me I had been designated a saboteur. He gave me a certificate of saboteurship. I was to hide it on my person until I got to the flag pole and then display it to the pole commander, simultaneously announcing that I had captured the flag. If I did that, then I would win and the flag defenders would lose. If I were captured, I would be held in prison until the end of the game. The game would end when the flag was taken or 2100 hours, whichever came first. The game which had not then been announced would be announced at supper a few weeks hence and begin right after announcement. Game rules had been prepared and were disclosed a few days thereafter. It was also stated that saboteurs would be selected shortly. Of course, that was a smoke screen. I had already been selected. I assumed that every other saboteur had also already been selected. And a good thing too because everyone was very watchful. The camp staff made special display of meeting with some campers, but not me. Whether any of them were designated, all of them denied it.

Before the appointed time, I went with Bert, my most forgetful friend, to the craft house on the outskirts of camp. We were beyond earshot of the loud speaker and would not hear the announcement of the game. I finished a lantern I had begun a few days before. That was the occasion for our departure.

Bert and I were heading back across the wheat field toward our cabin when we were accosted by a marauding group of flag defenders.

"Are you saboteurs?" Jason, their leader asked.

"Oh, has that game begun?" I responded.

"No," Bert chimed in. "We forgot."

"We were at the craft house." I lifted my lantern from my chest and smiled. "Let's go around and see if we can spot anyone sneaking around." With that Bert and I joined the group. We were lucky. We did spot Terry and after a short chase—I was the fastest—we grabbed him. When asked, he confessed that he was a saboteur. It amazed me that he would run, a sure sign of guilt and then confess. I did not show it, however. But, of course, that he was a saboteur would have been impossible to conceal after the message had been discovered. It was in the leather lining of his cap. Robby had retrieved it when it had flown off during Terry's flight. Robby discovered it in courteously handing Terry back his cap. Terry was not known to wear caps. He had never worn one at camp before. That made me think he must be a decoy. But again no one thought he was very bright.

I joined the contingent taking Terry to jail. It was in the mess hall not 100 feet from the flag pole. When we entered, we did so triumphantly, thinking we had been the first to make

4

a capture. However, other patrols had been as efficient. There were two other captured saboteurs in jail. Another came in and I assisted in checking him out. He was clean. He was appointed a jailer.

An hour passed. The jailers grew restless. They wanted to patrol or guard the pole. Just before Billy, an emissary from the pole commander, had come in to propose an exchange. As I had been on patrol and jailer from sometime, I volunteered for the pole.

"Everyone going to the pole has to be searched," Billy announced. I was not prone to reddening. Also, I was well tanned. I was not prone to perspiring or startlement. And I did not react, except to wonder if there had been any tell tale sign. Immediately upon that wonder, I was soothed in the satisfactory thought that I had been selected no doubt because of my phlegmatic demeanor and unemotional solution oriented approach to all crises. Robby was stripped first without result. Mike was next. He too was clean.

I took off everything. When I exposed my soles, Jason shouted "what's that" "His bandage," Bert blurted. "Ugh, it's bloody and full of puss." I dared to twist and look down. "My wound must have opened when I ran after Terry tonight. It hurt at first, but then with all the excitement, I forgot about it."

Everyone remembered that I had cut my right foot on a piece of glass in the creek a couple weeks ago, that I had gone to the infirmary for some stitches, I had told them, and that I had gone back periodically to get it looked at and get the bandage changed. I had also limped about a little now and again.

Nothing more was said. I got dressed and we went out to relieve the pole defenders, the changing of the guard.

The defense was more boring than the jail guarding. There was an outer perimeter to capture any saboteur who attempted to streak toward the pole like a suicide bomber.

Boris had waited in the woods until dark, when he slipped into the lake and swam under water, his snorkel barely exposed. Only in the last few yards out of the water onto the sand and up the grassy knoll to the pole would he be exposed.

At about 2045 hours there was a great splashing such as we had often heard when the Canadian geese ascended from the lake and into flight. The outer perimeter fixed on Boris coming out of the water. They descended on him at the bottom of the hill, shooting.

There was no need to ask if he was a saboteur or to look for his certificate. It would have been too dark to read anyway. His was a suicide mission, but he had come the closest.

As the last moments ticked off with each pole guard regaling each other in the glow of their successful defense and congratulating Boris on his daring attempt, I stepped forward.

I announced with as much cere-
mony as the occasion demanded:

"Jason, I am presenting my cre-
dentials as a saboteur." I reached
down, pulled the saboteur certificate
out from my bloody, pussy bandage. I
proffered it. Jason was too dumb
founded and disbelieving to move.

"I have captured the flag. Pull it
down. It is mine."

II

Of course there had been no flag.
That was hyperbole. It had been re-
tired ceremoniously before the game
began. At camp's end, however, Merriam presented my own miniature
flag. I kept it properly folded and in
its bag thereafter, except for occasion-
al display or when telling how I had
captured it, and until Congress went
crazy, declaring that the flag was a
living thing and that its mistreatment
was a crime. I did not want to have an
inanimate object about that could even
possibly result in criminal charges

against me or my family by some perverted patriot with an axe to grind against me, so I burned it in our furnace and vowed never to possess an American Flag again. I was not about to let the American flag capture me.

III

Later, the Supreme Court declared Congress' flag burning law unconstitutional. This did not alter my pledge never to possess any American flag. Quite the contrary. Flag burning was now lawful, subject, of course, to laws against destruction of government property, other property destruction offenses, and civil liability therefor. Also, the Supreme Court, being more political than judicial, reverses itself too frequently to rely on anything. What it says in one term, it can reverse the next. "Stare decisis" could easily melt as "stare de-ices." Also, who knows what the courts would do if some enterprising prosecutor brought a criminal case after such reversal with respect to a burning that had occurred other than in the interim that the unconstitutionality was effective. It is a possibility, given the Court's crazy quilt of *ex post facto* and retrospectivity analysis.

VI

By that time I had become fairly disgusted with the mean hypocrisy that the flag represented anyway and had no need of it. For me it symbolized the ugly American whom the world hated. I preferred to travel under the guise of a Swiss or a Scot, keeping my mouth shut. There are numerous other favored nationalities, but I do not possess the physiognomy or language to pass for them. The practice was of ultimate benefit. Hatred for the American increased as US interfered in their affairs and its history of butchery became common knowledge among the Peoples of the world. Ever after any American flag coming into the family was summarily destroyed. Every effort was made to keep it from the children's thoughts and activities.

V

I had before then harbored resentment against the flag, as if it really were a living being that one could dislike, even hate. I was used to mindlessly pledging allegiance to the flag every morning at school, at scout meetings and elsewhere. But one day and thereafter "under god" was added and, after some short period of bafflement and inquiry, I stopped pledging. God to me was a private matter. What is worse so much destruction, oppression and evil had been perpetrated in his name that I was not about to condone transformation of the flag into his aegis. So shortly after Congress added "Under God" to the Pledge, probably July 4, 1954, I stopped pledging altogether. It was not a personal decision because the public school I was attending stopped.

The principal was piqued. He could not have the local clergy on a rotating basis deliver the invocation at commencement and prayer on other ceremonial occasions. If any treatment of religions in sociology and history classes was "Verboten," he would take his revenge on the Pledge. Also, the flag was no longer flown or displayed at the school.

VI

In fact, it was at this school that I first became aware of the American flag as a symbol of mean hypocrisy. The flag was a symbol of revolt in a civilized colony from a civilized monarchy from which all of America's civilization and civility had descended. Britain was the force that had limited the further expansion into the Native Americans' territories by the treaty of 1763, which ended the French and Indian Wars. The federal government was the force that invaded Canada and later Mexico without provocation and solely to garner territory. Its incursions were thoroughly rebuffed from Canada with the aid of Britain. Not so, Mexico, which gave up substantial territorial claims. The federal government scammed Spain out of Cuba and Florida, the latter for itself. The federal government dictated removal of other nations from the hemisphere and interfered in other nations' affairs to destabilize other countries' economies in order to spread democracy in cultures where it could not take any but troublous root. In this, it was no better than the missionaries who spread the nonsense of the Holy Ghost and original sin, pestilence, disease and perverse alien cultures with the result of destroying paradise around the world. In this it was no better than the Communist scourge that replaced more paternalistic and caring governance with a ruthless machine without soul that promised an impossible dream premised on a topsy-turvy hierarchy and unnatural economics. As such conduct was alien to its avowed principles, hence conducted clandestinely, it was worse than either the Christian missionaries or the Communist comrades, a mean spirited land grabbing hypocrisy.

VII

The American States enslaved primitive Blacks and slaughtered the indigenous Indians, whom they could not enslave, all for their land, cotton and expansion beyond the treaty bounds. The federal government slaughtered its own in violation of the States' obvious legal right to secede from that which they and their citizens had voluntarily joined. The federal government emasculated the States, the People and other nations by bribing their leaders and making promises that would not be kept, invariably with disastrous result for those who the federal government purported to relieve from their shackles. For the federal government always abandoned those it purported to support at precisely the point of commitment when there could be no turning back, thus plunging them into certain captivity, even decapitation, legitimately as revolutionaries and traitors, at the hands of their extant governments.

VIII

The flag has been captured; its stars become wishful thinking, its stripes oppressive bars; its colors: red-blood; white—incendiary smoke and deceptive depiction of more holy than thou purity; and blue—pain and death by strangulation!

IX

They are at the pole pretending to guard the flag as a symbol for life, liberty and the pursuit of happiness. However, they are the saboteurs of the very life, liberty and the pursuit of happiness that the flag is supposed to represent for America, for the World. They were at the pole when I was an innocent child playing that game at camp and long before.

X

I do not know if there can be a just and honorable nation. What I do know is that the hypocrisy that goes by the name "United States of America" is not it. What I do know is that the flag as a symbol for such a nation has been discredited repeatedly from inception and throughout its history. What I do not yet know is whether those who are at the pole realize what they are guarding and why. That is the mission of a lifetime. For if they act out of ignorance, they can be educated; and if they act knowingly, and if that can be proven, they are criminals who may be prosecuted and punished.

➢

ABOUT THE AUTHOR

George Hook was born in Chicago. His education includes Junior Hall, Budlong Elementary School, and Junior Military Academy in Chicago, the Missouri Military Academy, in Mexico, Missouri, Knox College in Galesburg, Illinois, where he majored in English Composition and Political Science, the University of Chicago Law School, the Armor Officer School at Fort Knox, Kentucky, and the Judge Advocate General's School in Charlottesville, Virginia. He served three years in the US Army Judge Advocate General's Corps after graduation from law school, including a tour in Viet Nam. Thereafter, he returned to Chicago and practiced law. In college and throughout his career, he has written short stories and poetry. Several of his short stories were published in the "Siwasher,"[1] now renamed "Catch" in obeisance to political cor-

---

[1]Originating out of *At Old Siwash,* by George Fitch, K 1897.

rectness.[2] Vowing to eschew finalization of his literary works until he was of such an age as to have experienced life to the full, he began that process to culminate in publication upon his retirement from professional life. Currently, he is broadening his horizon to book length works of fiction and non-fiction.

---

[2]Believing "Siwash" to be a pejoration of American Indians of the Chinookian Tribes of the Northwest.

www.ingramcontent.com/pod-product-compliance
Lightning Source LLC
Chambersburg PA
CBHW070757120626
46557CB00002B/635